ENRICH SPOT

Published by

Enrich Spot Limited
A member of Enrich Culture Group
Unit A, 17/F, 78 Hung To Road,
Kwun Tong, Kowloon,
Hong Kong
Copyright © 2021 by Enrich Spot Limited
With the title *Giraffe and the Rain*
Story by Crisel Consunji & LeonLollipop
Lyrics & Music by Crisel Consunji
Music arrangement by Stephanie Chan
Illustrations by LeonLollipop

Edited by Zeny Lam
Book design by Elaine Chan

ISBN 978-988-75704-6-2

Published & printed in Hong Kong.

♪ Sing-along Storybook 01 ♪

Giraffe and the Rain

By Crisel Consunji
& LeonLollipop

Giraffe found a seed on a sunny day,
Went out with snail to go plant and play.

Dig, Dig, Dig,
Pop the seed into
the hole…
Wait, Wait, Wait,
'til it
Grows, Grows, Grows…

But then, Golden Sun
hid behind the clouds.
Rain started falling,
and falling down.

'Quick!' said Giraffe.
'Let's save the seed from
this awful rain!'

Howling and blowing,
raining and pouring...
Drip-drop, drip-drop,
drip-drop...

Raining and pouring,
howling and blowing,
Oooh- ooh - oooh-
ooh-ooooh...

Giraffe tried so hard to
protect the little seed.
'I give up,' said Giraffe.
'This seed will never
become a plant.'

Dear Giraffe,
It's alright to cry.
The rain will
stop someday…
You will get by.

Snail said,
'Who knows?
Maybe something
good will come out of
this rain.'

And then,
Golden Sun dried the rain away.
What do you think
happened on that day?

Mama said,
'Hey Giraffe,
look at your plant.
After the rain, sun will shine on the land.'

You thought the rain
would wash out the seed.
But both sun and rain
are what you need.

OH! It looks like
a lollipop!

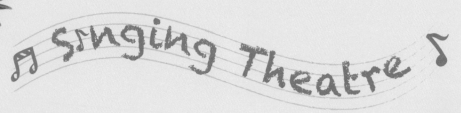

♫ Singing Theatre ♪

Giraffe

Snail

Narrator
(The character who tells you
what is happening in the story.)

Mama

Welcome to the Singing Theatre. Are you ready to get started?

♪ Invite your family or friends to sing with you.

♪♪ Have everyone pick 1 or 2 character(s) that they are going to sing their dialogue.

♪♪♪ Use maracas or other shakers to beat out a tempo, and shake harder when the rain comes, turning the whole book into musical!

Feelings Detective

Can you tell how Giraffe feels by looking at his face? Match **'Happy'** and **'Sad'** to the faces.

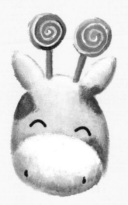 

How do you know Giraffe is really happy… or sad? What are the clues?

Happy	**Sad**
♪ Smile and laugh loudly?	♪ Sob?
♪ Skip around and dance?	♪ Being quiet?

Feelings can show up in many different ways – Tears don't always mean sadness and you can be excited quietly. There is no right or wrong. All these expressions are perfectly fine!

Sharing Time!

Like Giraffe, we all go through lots of different emotions every day. However you feel, it is always healthy to share your feelings. Let's act out the emotions using facial and body expressions, and say it with a reason!

Mummy took me to the park. I feel like sliding down a rainbow!

My favourite toy is broken. I feel like crying.

I feel happy when I play with my best friend.

My friend is moving away. I feel very sad.

I love taking my dog on walks around town.

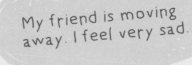

I am really upset because I dropped my ice cream.

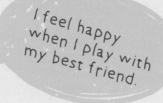

Feelings Museum

Write down your happy and sad moments. And try to let the happiness grow and blow the sadness away.

'Cultivation needs tremendous patience and determination that makes you see obstacles as great challenges—as a storm passes, we will see the beautiful rainbow at the best moment with the "best me". *Giraffe and the Rain* is a fun, musical book for children to enjoy the witty words but it also serves to cultivate our little children with a BIG heart.'

— Catherine Chan, A mother, published author and consulting editor

Crisel Consunji is an award-winning actress, singer, early years educator and community advocate. She has built a career on connecting and impacting lives through creative expression. In 2015, she founded Baumhaus, Hong Kong's first creative-arts based family centre, and continues to build programs and train families and early childhood educators in arts-based education. She has two Master's degrees—one in Political Science, and one in Early Childhood Education. She is active in community initiatives that support children, youth and family well-being, and her projects reflect her commitment to socially relevant causes.

🌐 www.criselconsunji.com

LeonLollipop (Leon Lai) is a multi-disciplined artist and gallery founder, who focused on animals painting. He graduated from Central St. Martins College of Arts and Design in the U.K. and he received a D&AD design award in London. Leon has launched his first illustration book in 2012, and followed by 4 children illustration storybooks, as well as many other crossover projects with international brands. You may find his artworks in hospital, hotel, restaurants, and cinemas in and also outside Hong Kong!

🌐 www.leonlollipop.com

To know more about Crisel and Leon, please scan